Eels

Written by Jack Gabolinscy

fins

Eels are fish.
They are long.
They look like snakes,
but they have fins.

2

This eel lives in the sea.

salt water

Eels live in the water.
Some eels live in the sea.
Some eels live in rivers
and lakes.

These eels live in a lake.

fresh water

muddy water

This eel likes to
live in muddy water.
It has a brown back.

clean water

This eel likes to
live in clean water.
It has a black back.

Some eels are short and
some eels are long.
Some of them are fat and
some are very, very fat!
Eels are not all the same.

0   6
                        feet

9

eel

Eels hunt for their food
in the water.
They have a lot of
very sharp teeth.
They eat little fish,
snails, and worms.

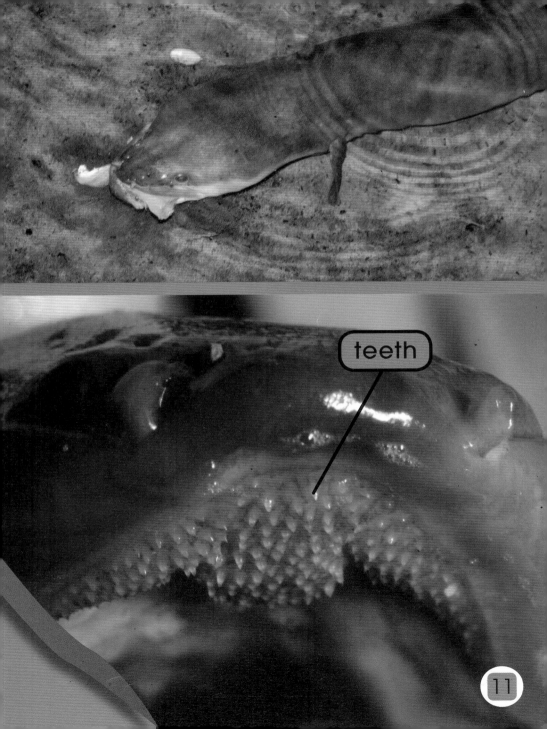

teeth

trap

Some people like
to catch eels and eat them.
They hunt for eels with
traps and spears.

spear

This man has made a big fire.
He puts the eels
over the fire to cook them.
The people will
buy these eels to eat!

Index

Guide Notes

Title: Eels
Stage: Early (3) – Blue

Genre: Nonfiction
Approach: Guided Reading
Processes: Thinking Critically, Exploring Language, Processing Information
Written and Visual Focus: Photographs (static images), Index, Labels, Captions, Scale Diagram
Word count: 149

THINKING CRITICALLY
(sample questions)

- Look at the front cover and the title. Ask the children what they know about eels.
- Read the title to the children.
- Focus the children's attention on the index. Ask: "What are you going to find out about in this book?"
- If you want to find out about cooking eels, which page would you look on?
- If you want to find out about where eels live, which pages would you look on?
- Look at page 6. Why do you think the eel likes to live in muddy water?
- Look at pages 12 and 13. How else do you think people could catch eels?

EXPLORING LANGUAGE

Terminology
Title, cover, photographs, author, photographers

Vocabulary
Interest words: eel, fins, rivers, muddy, traps, spears
High-frequency words: them, very, these
Positional words: in, over

Print Conventions
Capital letter for sentence beginnings, periods, commas, exclamation marks